"Can I have a red coat or a fluffy coat?" asked Bobbie.

Bobbie and Mom went to look
at the coats.
Mom looked at some red coats.
Bobbie looked at some fluffy coats.

Bobbie saw a fluffy coat.

"I like it!" said Bobbie.

"I like it, too," said Mom,

"but it's too big.

All the fluffy coats are too big."

Bobbie saw a red coat.

"I like it!" said Bobbie.

"I like it, too," said Mom,

"but it's too little.

All the red coats are too little."

"So I can't have a fluffy coat,"
said Bobbie.
"And I can't have a red coat."

Then Mom saw some red and blue
and yellow coats.
"Look at these coats, Bobbie,"
said Mom.
Bobbie put on a coat.

"I like it!" said Mom.
"Do you like it, Bobbie?"

Bobbie said, "Y-Y-Y-Yes."

Mom said, "We will take this coat."

Bobbie went to school
in her new coat.

She saw Carlos and Tilly.

"I've got a new coat!" said Bobbie.

"So do I!" said Carlos.

"So do I!" said Tilly.